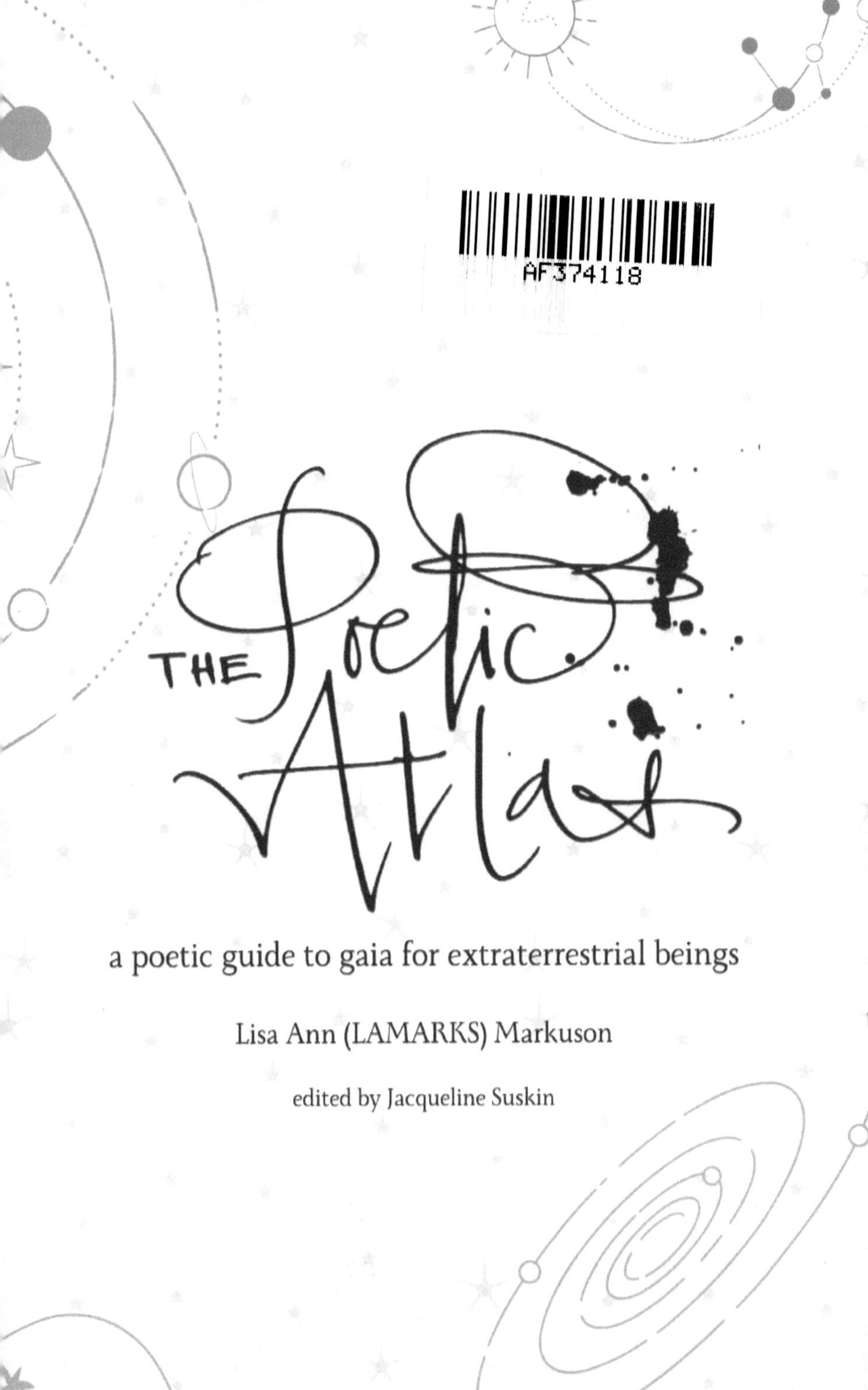

THE Poetic Atlas

a poetic guide to gaia for extraterrestrial beings

Lisa Ann (LAMARKS) Markuson

edited by Jacqueline Suskin

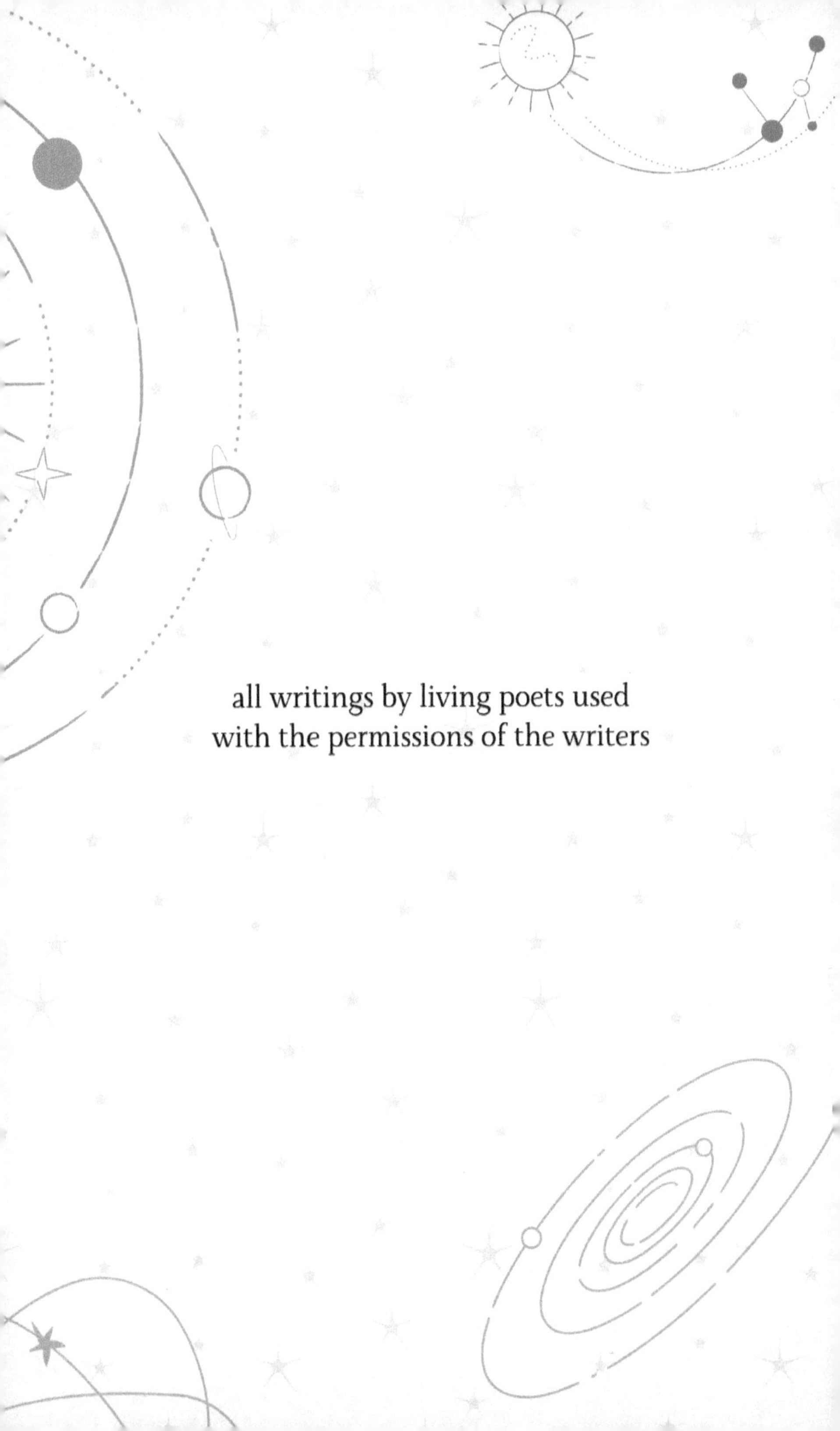

all writings by living poets used
with the permissions of the writers

The Poetic Atlas

Lisa Ann (LAMARKS) Markuson

2026

Nembrotha Books

Wayward Writers Press

Introduction & Invocation

For I could not find my audience on earth,
So I began to address my poems to the stars.

-LAMARKS

By the time you read this, it might be too late.
Or perhaps, as I am re-membering, we will realize that, like all things, it was right on time.

It is not up to me to decide. Time is not what we have been taught.

Poets are called upon to rise and make ourselves known in times of great need.
Yet we poets prove ourselves quite hard to find.

We change our monikers, our handles. We lose our phones. We do not turn in to the Post Office a notification of a change of address. We may not even have an address.

We modify our bodies and identities until even our relatives may find us hard to recognize.

If you happen to find an active email address, you will receive a cryptic away message or auto-responder. We may read your message, but it will not find us well.

Un-googlable, we fancy ourselves free. Free to eke out a living under empire, free to burst ourselves into flames, free to fight for or flee from a sliver of attention, or free to die in obscurity: self-sabotaged, censored, erased, devalued, and alone.

Case in point: myself. At the time of writing (New Year's Eve, 2025, 2:52pm EST) I have been looking for myself ceaselessly for 38 years, 359 days, 14 hours and 52 minutes. I seem to have found enough of myself to get these words of blue ink onto the yellow legal pad before me at my dining table, but there is still much, much more of me to discover.

And discover poets, we must. All of us.

For some reason (ask yourselves, the stars) I find myself called not only to discover this poet (me) and reveal her glory to the world, but also to use this little matchstick light of mine to shine, shine, shine *on the world.* For some, it is much to their chagrin. For others, there is enjoyment in the coloring of their cheeks and the opening of their palms. We are the lucky ones, we who can let the light in when the cracks appear.

The world, which I call Gaia, is calling urgently for poets to reveal ourselves. Apparently the hour is upon us when the bell demands to be rung another way. An apocalyptic ecosystem screams for us to heed her will lest we drown, burn, suffocate, or be crushed in her rubble as she makes way for the next phase of her evolution. If we cannot or will not ring the bell in our Lifeshines, we must at least rise to her command to tend to her cracks so some future generation may do the ringing. The unified resonance we long for, we know, will not weave itself forth from our unintentional cacophony of living. Oh no. Effort must be present, as well as imagination, for freedom to truly ring.

Liberty, like Gaia, is not an easy woman to please. We must weave something beautiful from the dirt and consciousness she hath so lovingly provided us. Provided to us, asking only in return that we might share it, and enjoy it, and grow and fight and rise and love together, as all Life must.

Notice in my list of things we must do, ways we must become, I did not write "give unto Caesar," nor has it been written that we must die. These, as it turns out, are not obligatory things, at least not to Gaia and the Laws of Life. Through poetry, in Unity, all things find their infinite flow. Just as you and I have found each other. Across galaxies.

So, herein will you find:

- A brief introduction to Life on Gaia and poetry as the most valuable and infinitely renewable resource and technology on this planet
- A pinprick primer on ancient Gaian poetry and the origins of poetic co-creation among homo sapiens sapiens
- 23 poetic stars in my personal constellation to whom I owe some of my light and whose revelation to you in this novel way will positively impact the unfolding of your Lifeshine
- Letters from and conversation with Gaia, and an appendix full of poetic Starshine Self-Relation for you to engage with in any way you so choose

Now, a final note on for whom I write.

Firstly, this book, The Poetic Atlas, is written for an audience of extraterrestrial beings. For aliens, angels, planets in this and other solar systems, all ascended and ascendant entities who mean well for Gaia and for Life, and of course for the stars themselves, I write. I write especially for our dear and charming Sun. I know it defies the poetic stereotype for me (a poet and a woman no less!) to dedicate my opus to the Sun and thereby put in second place her shy lover the moon. But I am not here to uphold stereotypes or expectations. I am here to shine my poetic light upon the world at the exact frequency I was given, so look elsewhere for apology!

Secondly, the book's physical paper form is devoted entirely to Gaia herself, from whence she hath come. I trust you will take care and not allow this copy that you steward to end up in a landfill. A landfill is the only place where she would never be able to reunite with herself and be born again. Share the book, scribble in her margins, dog-ear and recycle her pages, shred and compost her.

Third, I write for you, poetry-curious terrestrial being. Those times I could have given up, I did not, and I carried forward in this earthly avatar because I felt you and what our exchange of energy and ideas might reveal and unlock, and what we might experience. So much is possible, including the highest maximum pleasure together. Including even Unity and plenty among all stakeholders, first Life on this planet and then... everywhere else.

Lastly, and most importantly, I write for God. The God of Love who lives inside each of us and is so much greater than anything we could comprehend. The God who inspires and fuels all of our greatest poets and teachers. The God who shines this light on us so that we may find our way, together.

A brief introduction to Life on Gaia, and poetry as the most valuable renewable resource and technology on this planet

In the beginning there was the word.
And the word was light.

The Origin Story of All Life on Gaia

As channeled by Brent Thomas Asseff to LAMARKS

The origin story of our love and all Life on this earth is this:
A fleck of stardust from an infinitely distant star system enters a portal
And exits in the center of the earth,
Once it feels safe enough to come out

Because all Life is created with an urge to realize movement,
When it feels safe enough to move from its original position,
It can begin to perceive the power of the light of the Sun

Not only that - it can then hear the call of the Sun beckoning to draw nearer
The Sun and the stars say:

> Come to me, come to me
> In my light, in my warmth
> You will know the generative qualities of knowing
> That you are capable of being a source of power much like mine

And so Life journeys farther to a place
Where the world is more dry than wet
And yet the sense of safety remains
The light of the Sun envelopes it in a protective sphere
Even more protective than what darkness creates

From this vantage point
When the shine of the Sun becomes too much even for these brave
eyes
Life looks to the side
Where it unexpectedly finds other eyes also seeking the blessing
And eternal protection of the Sun

In that moment we realize that
Until now, we were alone
And now we are together
And it feels so good.

***

Now a time came that we wanted to move more. We wanted to
move ourselves, but where?

And why ever for?

We wanted to move to experience something new.

We wanted to mate, and we wanted to fight. Stakeholders, we
wanted to become.

In order to move toward new and pleasurable sensations and
activities, we had to develop our awareness.

We had to speed up and differentiate the way in which we
communicated our impulses.

So we began to listen.

Listening was wonderful, and it used a lot of energy. We liked the
feeling of using energy to listen, so we began to store energy inside
of ourselves so that we could use it whenever we wanted it.

And as we listened and moved and collected and stored energy,
of course there came a time when we dreamed. So much energy
needed an avenue of expression beyond what our consciousness
could provide. And we dreamed of not just any old thing, but
dreamed about the harvesting and storing and holding and using
of the energy of light in new and more powerful ways than only
when the Sun shone. We wanted light, at night.

And lo and behold, whether bless or cursing it was light we wanted and light we would have, first in the form of fire and then many many more ways, but fire is still our favorite.

Now, moving listening dreaming and light bearing as we were, some new need made itself known to Gaia. The need to speak.

But before we could speak, we had to learn to make ourselves known.

Learning, learning we went, making sounds with our bodies over and over until a new pattern emerged (or an old one was broken). I said one thing, and you said another. I liked the way you made your sounds, and you liked my sounds too. Those who could listen well and make good sounds were very powerful and valuable then. The listeners and talkers were the most valuable of all. And we were the best at fighting and mating, too.

And so, feeling, moving, dreaming, bearing light, learning, listening, speaking, fighting and mating, things became pretty exciting for us. So much so that we started to think.

Thinking was a bit of a problem, but we made it work, and it had its benefits.

From thinking came conscious memory, the awareness of being aware, the sapiens to our sapiens, and then of course the need to remember and to be remembered. A very energy intensive thing.

And as of now Life had grown and evolved so much that there were many of us feeling, moving, fighting, mating, listening, speaking and even thinking. And so we needed a way to grow our memory a LOT.

So we took our light to the limbs of a tree and we made a fire.

We sacrificed a smaller, not-talking being, and we gathered around our night light fire and cooked and ate the being, absorbing and being fueled by the light we made and all the light the being had ever consumed. This powerful ritual and the heartbeat we shared fueled us to make a rhythm upon which our huge memory could dance. Dance to all of the rhythms and sounds that we made with our lights and our shadows.

We made music.

And in the music was poetry. And in our bodies was light. And the poetry in the music crystallized and structured our memory so powerfully, so gracefully that soon we wanted to share even more memory. More memory couldn't fit inside of our bodies so we began to look for a way for our memories to leave our bodies but continue to be with us.

We began to write.

Writing was our first intentional act of perfection, or transcendence. It was the allowing of our feelings to liberate themselves from our bodies and live forever in our consciousness, in our environment.

And around these written memories, societies formed. And around these societies, hierarchies, laws, and orders. And around these orders, empires crystallized, further disembodying our feelings from our physical forms and turning them into fuels of all kinds.

In our empires we have focused on burning the fuels of dead things. But the heartform of poetry is living fuel.

In empires, poets are born.
Empires must produce poetry.
And poetically, empires fall.

Notes on the technologies of language

And the Word was made flesh,
and dwelt among us, full of grace and truth.

Homo sapiens sapiens, now in possession of this fundamental
tool of communication via vocalized and embodied symbolism aka
language, needed to fuss with it. We could have called ourselves
homo sapiens *fuss-on-allens*, because to fuss upon everything we
create seems to be the main focus of our aware of being awareness.

Once we could draw attention to ourselves, and were able to
compel others to notice and attend to things we believed to be
important, we wanted more and more of it. Attention is addictive,
come to find out, and addiction is all-encompassing.

We had an attention economy from long before the term, or
probably any terms, became known to us. Look at me. See me.
Want me. Love me. Know me.

I won't bore you (or myself) with a lengthy technical manual of
the many fascinating inventions we homo sapiens sapiens have
invented, wielded, created and destroyed over the aeons, but I'll
leave you with these notes on what I see as the most monumental
advances in our communications technologies. Please do research
further in your own planet or galaxy, and feel free to compare
them with any of the comms tech your Lifeforms have invented on
your planet.

On Rhythm

Rhythm is the sixth sense. Rhythm is the building block of
memory.

On Memory

Only Life has memory. There is no memory without Life.

On Purpose

Memory creates purpose for Life. Only Life has purpose, and the purpose of Life is re-membering love.

On Ritualized Plant Relationship

To re-member love, we nurture those that hold, transform and share the light: plants. We relate with plants to fuel, adorn, heal, entertain, open, protect, warm, and help us feel aligned with our rhythm, memory, and purpose. Plants take on a symbolic power as they are our source of material resilience. We communicate with plants, and they with us.

On Performative Narrativized Storytelling

After language and consciousness, memory and purpose, the most important and often overlooked technology of communication is performative, narrativized storytelling. This is how homo sapiens sapiens became capable of collective societal evolution. And while every community group needs expert performative narrativized storytellers who can rally and direct the spirit of our consciousness, every participant in the society must develop this technology within themselves as well. The total centralization of performative narrativized storytelling to agents of the state, commerce, religious leadership, or even just the head of the family will inevitably cause a collapse in the society. Every single participant in the evolution of homo sapiens sapiens must be able to confidently tell their own story, understand its development and impact, and surrender, commit to, and believe in its important role in the collective story. This is inherent to the evolution of Life on Gaia.

On Archetypes

Before there was psychology, there were archetypes. Archetypes are a sociolinguistic categorization tool that aids in the exploration and development of every individual participant and the collective Life force on the planet. Know your role, along with its strengths and weaknesses, its offerings and its needs, and be able to develop

with confidence to become an empowered stakeholder in your
community group. These are the basic archetypes: entry points
to stakeholding. There are infinite more subtle subcategories and
blends of archetypes. Once you have developed successfully and
with confidence as an individual and member of the collective, you
can release your archetype and evolve into further Unity, if you so
choose.

1) The Mother / Life-Giver
2) The Elder / Ancestor-Keeper
3) The Child / New Beginning
4) The Healer / Restorer
5) The Trickster / Pattern-Breaker / Portal Maker
6) The Hunter / Provider
7) The Warrior / Protector
8) The Lover / Weaver
9) The Seer / Dreamer
10) The Steward / Leader

On Notes

Notes are small containers to organize and direct meaning,
purpose, rhythm, archetypes and stories. Notes allow words to be
exchanged between specific stakeholders. Notes allow reference.

On Keys

Keys are categorizing tools that allow us to access new wavelengths
of awareness. Keys can be codes. Keys can be elements. Keys
can be passwords, spoken or unspeakable. Keys can change
frequencies, to weave new meaning from our poetry. Keys unlock
new possibilities.

On Mirrors

Mirrors are reflectors. Reflection is beautiful. Too much reflection
is blinding. Too much reflection can turn perception into
obsession, starlight into immolation, angels into fish, youth into
taxidermy. Reflection does need a mirror. Smashing a mirror will
not keep you from being seen.

On Naming

It is beautiful to name. In naming, there are no objects, only subjects. We name those subjects which we do not know. Once we know a subject, they may desire to make the name they give themself known to us. The name one gives oneself is one's true name. Every stakeholder has a say in naming.

On Spelling

For Gaia, to *spell* a word is the same as to *cast* a spell. Use of precise letters and words to convey specific and intentional meaning, is an invocation of terrestrial and cosmic powers to aid and elevate Life. To give away your ability to spell is to give away your ability to invoke your highest maximum pleasure together. To spell is to be free.

On Ink

First there was blood. Then there was berry. Then we came to know of even darker and brighter things with which we could consecrate our inventions to memory outside of our bodies, inside of stories. To have ink is a privilege. Spill not blood or berry or ink without need, without intentions from all stakeholders. What is in your ink matters.

On Paper

Homo sapiens sapiens fights over which of us deserves credit for inventing paper. In fact and fantasy, the plant and animal fibers we use deserve the credit. Do we think we could have started writing on clay tablets and grass and trees and sheepskins without their consent? Our hubris is astounding. I hope you do not have this problem in your star system. I call upon us to give gratitude and treat every piece of paper, stationery, vellum, note card, poster, letter and stamp like it is a precious gift to and from ourselves and our mother. Because it is.

On Poetry

A poem is a portal.
A jeweled kaleidoscope to peer through
  To find our way though the night is dark
A way to create new worlds with our words.
Trust a poem,
   open yourself up to your intuition
Immerse yourself in a linguistic utopia.
Where the only rules are feelings.
And all your feelings are free.

In poems, language does whatever it desires.
  Grammar? Who needs it?
  No punctuation? No problem.
A poem is a process, but it is also a destination.
Completed, a poem becomes
  a postcard of possibility
A reminder that things imagined can become real things.
  That we can trust ourselves and our ideas.
   We can transcend our limitations
And turn seemingly impossibly different dreams into colorfully
united realities.

On The Typewriter

I obsess over the typewriter and believe it is worth your specific
attention because of its Life at the intersection of technology
and embodiment. While typewriting is less embodied than, say,
dancing, as a form of communication technology appreciated
here and now in the 3rd, 4th, and 5th dimensions it allows
us to maintain a more grounded embodiment than any other
communication machine. While our ideas are translated via
electrical impulse from our heartmind to our fingertips, the letters
and words that we type still stay fully manual and analog as they
meet the page in the form of ink. Then, to be read, they are taken
up purely by the organic apertures of the homo sapiens sapiens'
eye, digested again into electrical impulses in the body of the
reader.

This is why the typewriter remains the most valuable and effective machine for poetic co-creation to this day. It brings about more embodiment and empathy as its frequency changes key but is not obliged to change its wavelength, therefore maintaining most of its energy and making a highly efficient, highly impactful transfer of emotion between writer, reader, and even third party onlookers. The only thing better is eye gazing, which can be a bit much for unaccustomed homo sapiens sapiens.

On the telegraph

But for the sake of this introduction suffice it to say that Gaia has no problem with the use of electricity for connectivity, entertainment, organization and overall Life support. The problem lies when there are not poets represented and a balance of archetypes overall in the creation of massive new technologies. Electricity and electronic communication are much more beautiful when co-created with contributions and mutual consent from all stakeholders.

On social and feed-based media

Homo sapiens sapiens has always desired telepathy. I want to be understood. So do you. That is beautiful. Understanding, overstanding, and innerstanding can only be accessed when there is mutual consent. Surveillance, censorship, data harvesting, algorithmic subconscious consciousness shifting, trolls, chatbot relationships, infotainment and advertising do not support mutual consensual understanding.

On machine learning and artificial general intelligence

The sharing of and collectivizing of information is beautiful. For the sharing and collectivizing of information to reach its highest maximum potential for beauty and pleasure, it must be done with mutual consent and equitable energy exchange among all those who give and receive the information.

If a branch of your tree is burned for warmth, so must you receive
a proportional quantity of light and heat from the burning of
that branch. And all stakeholders in the branch must consent
to the burning, and fully understand all of the implications of
that burning. And systems must be in place to process all of the
products and impacts of that burning and that light and that heat.

Do you understand?

This has been hard for us to understand, in any sort of Unified
manner.

The branch belongs to all of us, including the branch themself.

Poetic co-creation commands us: if all will burn and be burned
and feel the warmth and see the light and chemically transform
within that light, all must mutually consent to the liberation of that
beauty, and the application of that beauty toward the elevation of
collective consciousness.

Large language models as they are currently constructed will never
reach their highest maximum potential for the liberation of beauty
and elevation of collective consciousness because they have not
been constructed with mutual consent from all stakeholders.

Earn the consent of the creators and stakeholders, and the highest
possible outcome of the technology will effortlessly reveal itself to
all.

The poets are here to teach us this.

Let us see now where poets come from.

A pinprick primer on ancient Gaian poetry and the origins of poetic co-creation among homo sapiens sapiens

ENHEDUANNA

Lady of all the divine powers,
resplendent light,
who covers herself with terrifying brilliance.

You are the one who turns men into women
and women into men.

To turn a country into a wasteland,
to destroy it,
to crush it—
this is yours, Inanna.

I have given birth, O exalted lady,
to this song for you.

The first poet committed to our collective written memory is the Mesopotamian priestess Enheduanna, who was born over four thousand years ago, circa 2286 BC. She was the ultimate inheritrix of privilege, as close as you could be to a goddess in mortal flesh. She was the first person to acknowledge herself in her writing, in glyphs painstakingly pressed into clay tablets. She was the first person we know of who signed her poems. She is why I sign my poems.

She was born into immense wealth, in a politically tumultuous time. She helped two warring empires fuse, and brought spiritual leadership to a time of great geopolitical strife and confusion. She was exiled for a time, but restored to power soon after.

Her poems, often considered more like hymns, served a higher power. Her inspiration wove divergent populations together, and ushered in new forms of consciousness and creativity in the cradle of homo sapiens sapiens' civilization.

SAPPHO

That man seems to me to be equal to the gods
who is sitting opposite you
and hears you nearby
speaking sweetly

and laughing delightfully, which indeed
makes my heart flutter in my breast;
for when I look at you even for a short time,
it is no longer possible for me to speak

but it is as if my tongue is broken
and immediately a subtle fire has run over my skin,
I cannot see anything with my eyes,
and my ears are buzzing

a cold sweat comes over me, trembling
seizes me all over, I am paler
than grass, and I seem nearly
to have died.

The next eldest sister in our poetic lineage is Sappho, born in
650BC just a stone's throw away on the Isle of Lesbos, in present
day Greece. She also was a privileged and well endowed daughter
of wealthy parents. While not a political leader per se, she did sit
in a position of political power and was exiled at one time to
present day Sicily.

Credited with the creation and dissemination of the Sapphic
stanza, which changed the course of all classical poetry, it is
worthwhile to note that the lasting reputation of the prolific
poetess is queer feminine love and longing, with both her name
and the name of her home island, Sappho and Lesbos, being
inextricable and in fact the origin of two common words for the
love shared between women: sapphic and lesbian.

Sappho used her poetic power not just to express herself and
direct her audience's attention, but to evolve the possibilities and
containers of expression itself.

HORACE

Poets wish to benefit or to please, or to speak
What is both enjoyable and helpful to living.
When you give instruction, be brief, what's quickly
Said the spirit grasps easily, faithfully retains:
Everything superfluous flows out of a full mind.
Fictions meant to amuse should be close to reality,
So your play shouldn't ask for belief in whatever
It chooses: no living child from the Lamia's full belly!
The ranks of our elders drive out what lacks virtue,
The Ramnes, the young knights, reject dry poetry:
Who can blend usefulness and sweetness wins every
Vote, at once delighting and teaching the reader.
That's the book that earns the Sosii money, crosses
The seas, and wins its author fame throughout the ages.

And finally we meet our first noteworthy male poet, Quintus Horatius Flaccus (Horace), born in 65 BC in the heart of the Roman Republic, on the cusp of alchemizing itself into the Roman Empire. Born to parents once enslaved by the nascent empire, his father freed and elevated himself to some notable standing and wealth, spending hugely on the education of his gifted son.

He was taught in The Academy of Plato in Athens, and as the Roman Empire consolidated power his ancestral homeland was usurped by the Emperor and his military. But his fortunes improved when he found a wealthy patron to provide for him. The Roman Empire, as you can imagine if you have experienced any Empires in your galaxy, was pretty much always a moral, political, ethical, and environmental disaster, and many of Horace's poems entreated fellow citizens to just do better. Many of his works were also applied to empirical goals such as convincing colonized communities to submit to Roman rule. He went on to befriend and serve the Emperor directly, writing many poems celebrating Roman conquests, and of course his epistle *Ars Poetica*, convincing his readers of the infinite power of poetry to entertain and educate, to bring about catharsis as well as consciousness.

YESHUA of NAZARETH

"Woman, where are they? Has no one condemned you?"
"No one, sir," she said.

"Then neither do I condemn you," Jesus declared. "Go now and leave your life of sin."

Yeshua, or Jesus, a Palestinian refugee born to a teenaged mother who in all likelihood escaped some form of state oppression, abuse and victimization, was a great poet. And like most great poets of the ancient world, he was surrounded by many who would write and express with awe his poetic being, teaching, and miraculous poetic co-creation.

Born into abysmal circumstances during a politically violent, oppressive, and unstable time, there was almost no possibility for Jesus to become a recognized and respected figure in his community, let alone the entire world. But he did. How? It wasn't just because he befriended some wealthy patrons and grew his fandom, though he did do that and without them he certainly would not be remembered as he is.

So how then?

Jesus devoted his life completely to the conveyance of the liberating poetic truths and knowings of his heart.

Why is Jesus not renowned as the greatest poet of all time? There are many reasons, but here is one: he did not write. At least, not that we know of. He orated, he meditated, he healed, he inspired, he stimulated the emotions and creative capacity of all who experienced his presence, but unlike other ancient poets of great import to our collective conscience, we do not have in circulation his original words, written by his own hand.

There is only one instance in the Bible, our flawed but generally accepted reference point for documentation of the life and teachings of Jesus, when he was witnessed writing.

And no one seems to know what he wrote.

Not on paper, did he scribe, but in the sand beneath his feet, as if conjuring wisdom from Gaia herself as to how to guide an angry group of beings who desired to shame and punish a woman among them according to outdated laws desperate to be composted and co-created anew. After running his finger through the dirt, he said to the rageful wounded ones around him:

"Let any one of you who is without sin be the first to throw a stone at her."

And the crowd dispersed, and the woman was free.

What do you think he wrote with the earth?

Why do you think Gaia was forever changed by his poetry?

What divinity is channeled through the embodied words and living light of poets who dare to allow their messages to be written and read for thousands of years to come?

There is still much work to be done, if we are to bring about another arrival of what many of us refer to as Christ Consciousness, the love of the universe in every living being.

SAINT AUGUSTINE

I praise the dance, for it frees people
from the heaviness of matter
and binds the isolated to community.
I praise the dance, which demands everything:
health and a clear spirit and a buoyant soul.
Dance is a transformation of space, of time, of people,
who are in constant danger of becoming all brain,
will, or feeling.
Dancing demands a whole person, one who is
firmly anchored in the center of his life, who is
not obsessed by lust for people and things
and the demon of isolation in his own ego.
Dancing demands a freed person, one who vibrates
with the balance of all his powers.
I praise the dance.
O man, learn to dance, or else the angels in heaven
will not know what to do with you.

A few hundred years after Horace's death, another great
Mediterranean poet took his first breath in a southern outpost of
the Roman Empire: Augustine of Hippo in 354AD, in present-
day Algeria. Depicted in much classical art as a pale, bald man,
he was almost certainly Black, which may or may not have any
significance to you if in your star system there have not existed
systems of oppression that use the chemical makeup of one's
skin as a determining factor of one's value in the civilization, the
empire.

Continuing with our theme of privilege, spirituality, and
empirical sustenance in the face of catastrophic collective
collapse and creation, Augustine was a successful son of the
colonization of Africa by Rome. He came from religion and
resources, and continued the pursuit of material resilience and
spiritual satisfaction and the elevation of collective consciousness
throughout his Lifeshine. Just look at his devotion to the poetic
co-creation form known as dance. To dance is to move poetically,
with intention, grace and pleasure. To write a poem of dance, or to
dance to the frequency of poetry, is to use Gaian technology most
sacredly. It is to convert energy into love, and love into higher
forms of Unity.

Conversion is a major theme in the Life and work of Augustine, who chose to be baptised as a Christian and spent the rest of his Life using his rhetorical and dancing skills to bring others to his faith, now the official religion of the once pagan Roman Empire. Like all other ancient poets, he also lost his home, besieged by a Germanic tribe called the Vandals. Burning the entire city, the Vandals spared only Saint Augustine's library and cathedral from destruction, because even in the rage of battle known it was that a house of poetry is not to be desecrated. No Gaian Life would desecrate, devalue or demise a poet or poetry, Gaia's greatest resource, greatest technology. To this day Augustine is known as the patron saint of brewers, printers, and theologians. He enjoys this very much.

HILDEGARD VON BINGEN

We cannot live in a world that is not our own,
in a world that is interpreted for us by others.
An interpreted world is not a home.
Part of the terror is to take back our own listening,
to use our own voice, to see our own light.

Dare to declare who you are.

It is not far from the shores of silence
       to the boundaries of speech.
The path is not long,
       but the way is deep.
You must not only walk there,
       you must be prepared to leap.

Hildegard von Bingen was the tenth child of minor free nobility in
a remote forest in the northern Holy Roman Empire (what is now
present-day Germany). According to Gaian historians she does not
belong in my category of "ancient" but I remind, I follow only the
Laws of Life. As such, it was normal for her to be given as a tribute
of sorts to the empirical powers of the region. To consciously give
a young poet to the empire is a great gift indeed. She took her vows
and was enclosed in a feminine hermitage by the time she would
have had her first period.

A visionary from early childhood, Hildegard learned, worked, and
worshiped with great devotion and was loved by all. She was made
the magistra of her monastery, but sought more freedom from
the patriarchal rule of the church and so got permission from her
boss's boss to start a new smaller, more independent monastery
where she and other nuns could practice toward some form of
cosmic liberation without fear of persecution.

Her works are immense, radical, and divinely feminist, and
yet somehow avoided being condemned or seen as heretical.
Multiple popes read and blessed her visionary work. She also
wrote respected works of scientific and medical import, including
groundbreaking works on the curative powers of many plants
and animals and their "greening power" (*veriditas*) to heal homo
sapiens sapiens, God's creation, the world, Gaia.

She also invented, channeled, and documented her own language,
lingua ignota, or unknown language. She used her new technology
to bring about divine awarenesses heretofore unbeknownst to
her community, her very own empire. And somehow she was so
protected in the sharing of these truths, that even the emperors of
her realm did not want to destroy her.

She worked within a toxic system, and brought about beauty and
healing through poetic co-creation.

Hildegard von Bingen, St Augustine, Jesus, Horace, Sappho, and Enheduanna were some of Gaia's earliest seeds of higher collective consciousness fueled by language, filled with light. As empires grew and created more concentrated putrescence and Life's expression elevated its frequency, already was invoked the nature of Gaian poetry to collect, correct, and heighten our pleasure, our beauty, and the liberation of our bodies, minds, spirits and collective soul.

Ancient poets were the seeds that Gaia planted in the compost and sludge of Life and empire. Sprouted ideas, rooted identities, blooming embodiment, and fruits of re-memory. But dissonance still remained.

Blessed are we to have had at such an early stage in our evolution seeds of such green potency as these. And furthermore to not have burned them at the stake, as so many we know have been, in some such disintegrated courts where judge and judged do not hold the same stake of love.

I wish I could have known more of these poets.

What did they drink at sunset? What ancient instrument played their favorite tune? What did they gossip about? How did they like to be called by their friends?

What did they look like, really? What would they have thought of us now? What did they know and want to say but could not, as much as their sweetness and beauty in the empire was the line and lyric that held their Lifeshine aloft?

To know not the answers to these questions plagues me.

That the clear ringing of these bells was heard but not heeded over a thousand years ago is a great grief of my heart. This darkness in our collective memory keeps locked the door to the next phase of our evolution. And it is at Gaia's behest that I must learn these details from the poets currently living in this dimension, this plane, the moment, this place.

I must collect the names and secret knowings of Gaian poets now, and share this information with the stars.

Conclusions drawn from our tour through the ancient poets of Gaia

Now we see all Gaian poets of great collective import embody these: economic elevation, empire and exile, sensuality, spiritual service, education, and exoticism, or strangeness.

Successful poets are eloquent and attractive voices who call for the elevation of the collective consciousness of empire, not necessarily the destruction of it.

Poets are enthusiastic servants to pleasure and enlightenment.

Poets serve the wicked and bring them into Unity of consciousness.

Poets pour out their blood as spirit here to dissolve separation and bring about the conditions for poetic co-creation, the liberation of beauty, the attraction and selection of higher and higher frequencies of existence.

Poets thrive off of poison, turn it into compost, and press into Gaia's flesh the seeds of consciousness to sprout and root and blossom and bear fruit.

Poets throughout history have been fated to obscurity, censorship and deletion from our collective memory over time because words that do not contribute to empire are not allowed to resonate. But this does not have to be the case. Poets are seeds that must blossom and fruit new consciousnesses of many kinds. Some of us will use our tenacious roots to crumble the walls of the gardens in which we are planted. Others will feed the wolves who strike fear into the hearts of kings. Others will nurture babies born into free unwalled lands and some will nurse back to health the fallow fields. Some of us are mushrooms, fruiting in the dark. Others are Sunflowers, redwoods, cactus, kelp.

The only question is, poet: are you ready to leave your husk
behind, and sprout?

As each empire rises and falls, we feed a universal empress who
breathes more deeply and sings more sweetly. That empress is
Gaia. We are our mother earth. There is an empire that need never
fall or collapse.

We can become a planetary body pollinated by a cosmic suitor who
seeks to liberate our beauty with mutual consent.

The technology is poetry.
The process is poetic co-creation.
The destination is Unity.
The key is higher, and higher.
So now let us look at the constellation of poets
as I have encountered them until this juncture.

One more question:

Would you like to meet the poet avatars already sprouted
in Gaia's garden and in my awareness?

23 poetic stars in my personal constellation
to whom I owe some of my light & whose revelation to you
in this novel way will positively impact the unfolding of your
Lifeshine

This is not a Michelin Guide to poetry. (Have you heard of it?)
Though it could, over iteration and collective input, evolve
into something as aspirational and transformative as that, on
an intergalactic scale. Imagine a world, a universe where a
trustworthy body gives stars to poets and those stars signify a
certain power, a certain magnetism, a certain cultural import
worth currency in the composting empire? A Michelin Poem
alongside your Michelin meal, though hopefully no longer arrived
at by fossil-fueled automobile upon rubberized Michelin tires. In
its current first iteration, this is an atlas of a small sampling of the
poetic starlight that has guided me through the long dark night
of my soul's journey from conscious captivity to poetic liberation.
The light of these stars has created new worlds of Life in me, the
way the great poets of ancient times sprouted eyes in the hearts of
their empires.

The poets featured here have not only guided me with their
words, but with their whole beings. All of them dedicate at least
some part of their creative career and poetic practice to public
and collective service. That is crucially important for Gaia. All of
them demonstrate the characteristics of the great ancient poets.
All of them carry crucial keys and unique frequencies. Each offers
the embodiment of their words to the liberation of beauty and
in service to something greater, not merely their own Lifeshine.
Writing for the sake of auto-aggrandizement, standing on a stage
to see only the light of yourself, blooming not to share the fruit but
to hoard your seeds... this is not poetry. These are not poets, not to
Gaia. It is important to re-member ourselves as beauty liberated
united lifted up and felt fully, not beauty utilized to separate,
commodify, oppress, forget, or numb.

I do not know what history books from this time will survive, and certainly many of our digital archives are lost already, so I trust this atlas to do its work by impressing into the clay tablets of our minds, the collective Gaian and intergalactic memory, not just the names, poems, and countries of birth of these poets. This atlas also maps each poet's unique interdimensional coordinates in the tapestry of collective consciousness, on our journey toward the liberation of beauty via poetic co-creation. The keys of their secret knowings.

Visit their avatars here, read their words, follow their stories, wrap yourself in their wisdoms, sing their songs, and commit yourselves to each other guided by the nighttime fires of their hearts. Say their names out loud. Immerse yourself in the pleasure of hearing their words in your own unique voice.

Remember them.

Remember yourself.

Reignite the fire within.

Reflect the light out.

Plant their seeds, and let's feel what sprouts.

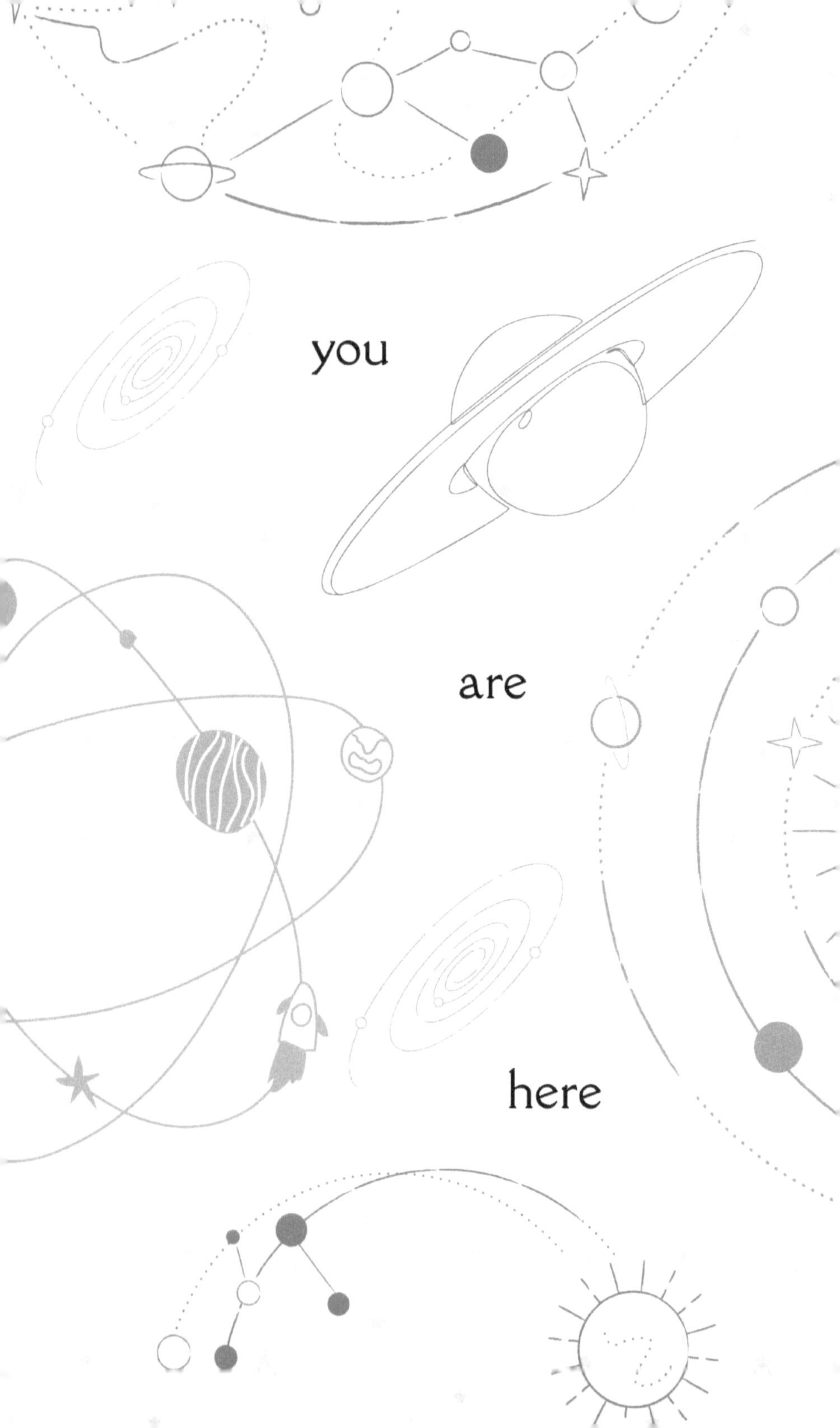

you
are
here

My Gaian Poet Constellation
In some particular order

1. Lisa Ann (LAMARKS) Markuson
2. shan noor hussein
3. Lauren Ducrey
4. Sabrina Cleary
5. ER Pulgar
6. Tevin Muendo
7. Eleonora Vaccari
8. Monique Marani
9. Juan Lli Pedraza
10. Brian Sonia Wallace
11. Mona Jean Cedar
12. Sasha Stiles
13. Jacqueline Suskin
14. Caridad De Le Luz
15. Bruce George
16. Bob Holman
17. Elizabeth Torres
18. E. Ethelbert Miller
19. Leasha Richards Miller
20. Britny Cordera
21. Crista Reid
22. Jane Potthast
23. Tania Asnes

Life Soundtrack

Enya
Annie Lennox
Sade
Sting

Values

sharing ~ unity
beauty ~ liberation
pleasure

SOLAR
RETURN
Jan 6 1987

Writing Influences

Gertrude Stein
Mark Twain
Octavia Butler
Ursula K. LeGuin

Vices

disdain for rules
rushing ~ forgetting
dirty martinis

childlike empress of poetic co-creation

Lisa Ann Markuson

Weapon of Choice

Chrome Hermes Baby
restored by El Granero

Self Care Ritual

sacred bathing ~
baptism

Planetary Alignments

Home Base:
Charlotte, NC

Most Poetic City:
San Francisco

Celestial Body:
Polaris

Iconic Accessory

Glasses
avante garde hairstyle

Community Care Ritual

mentoring young artists
donating poetic services

Superpowers + Talents

poetic co-creation ~ typewriter poetry ~ imagination ~ channeling ~ devotion

You're like good whiskey~
You're taking on the flavor
which sets you apart

-LAMARKS

Find Her:

@lisaannmarkuson // arspoetica.us

Life Soundtrack

Mereba
Meklit
Ensaf Madani
Noname
Chance the Rapper

Favorite Lost Cause

If we all moved slower and
acted with more intention,
more would actually get done

SOLAR
RETURN
April 22 1992

Writing Influences

June Jordan
bell hooks
Audre Lorde
Lucille Clifton
Alexis Pauline Gumbs

Power Flower

Hibiscus and/or
bougainvilleas

Weapon of Choice

Precise V5 Extra Fine
Rolling Ball Pilot pen
Typewriter

Self Care Ritual

Naming my
gratitudes out loud

Planetary Alignments

Home Base:
Unceded Ohlone territory as a
guest on Turtle Island & Poetic
nostalgia & Diasporic longing

Most Poetic City:
Kosti, Sudan

Celestial Bodies:
The Moon, Pluto,
Taurus and Pisces

Iconic Accessory

Always wearing
something white

Community Care Ritual

Praying at my altar
for those who need it

Superpowers + Talents

intuition, deep listening, time-space travel

My grandmother's kitchen

The Nile River

The porch of my
grandfather's home

Black
Buddhism

African
Traditional
Religions

Queer Black
feminist literature

what does it mean to seek joy,
and rest, and paradise
                for Black people in the end of times?
how will it feel? what will it look like?

i imagine moments of freedom
                strung together like the prayer beads
                              i offer to the ocean

i imagine no prisons or police or military - just vibes
i imagine everyone i love in one place even briefly
i imagine rest and creativity and growing with
every season
i imagine running water and loud birds and a dry
breeze
i imagine self care sunday everyday
and angels at my bedside
and you.

i imagine you.

                              -shah noor hussein

Find Them:

shahnoorhussein.com // IG: @ shah_noor // Substack: @ shahnoorwrites

35

Life Soundtrack

Shania Twain
(Man, I feel like a woman)
Hermanos Gutierrez
Grandbrothers
Niklas Paschburg
Stavroz

Writing Influences

The OG: Mary Oliver
Max Stossel
Lindsay Rush
(@maryoliversdrunkcousin)
David Whyte

Values & Superpower

Curiosity, Understanding, Silliness
& A podcast voice

Power Flower

Orange blossom

Weapon of Choice

Silky smooth ballpoint pen

Self
Care Rituals

Wandering without a
destination, buying food
on the way and cooking a
really delicious dinner

Planetary Alignments

Home Base:

In the soft center
of a fresh-baked baguette

Most Poetic City:

Santa Fe, NM

Celestial Body:

the atoms of carbon forged
in the bowels of stars
swirling in your body right now

Iconic Accessory

Two piece sets
with loud patterns.

Community
Care Rituals

Hosting open mics, especially
for folks who've never shared
their creativity out loud

Favorite Lost Cause

Unstarving the artist. Blaming financially successful poets as sell-outs only furthers the
neoliberal capitalist agenda of exiling the arts from current systems of value creation.

circle
back

I will circle back to your email
with the velvet curls
that nape a toddler's neck,
I will hit the ground running
like water from the tap in my bath,
I will kick off
my shoes and wiggle toes down
to the very end of my bed,
I will touch base with
the rug beneath my feat
and the pavement that I beat
southward from our North Star
because the sky is a gaggle of glimmers
that quack their light at me,
my ducks that are in anything but in a row.

-Lauren Ducrey

Find Her:

LinkedIn: Lauren Ducrey // laurenducrey.com

Life Soundtrack

Pearl Jam
Led Zeppelin
St. Vincent

Favorite Lost Cause

Being allowed to be

Power Flower

Coneflower

Writing Influences

Everything I've ever
read and forgotten

Embodiment

Solo intimacy

Competition

Athletics

Sabrina Cleary

Weapon of Choice

Pilot Precise V5 Retractable
Extra Fine Blue

Self Care Rituals

Reading before bed

Community Care Rituals

Making space

Planetary Alignments

Home Base:

The Margin

Most Poetic City:

Chippewa Township
Pennsylvania

Celestial Body:

A galaxy in formation

Iconic Accessory

Revolving notebooks

Favorite Form of Suffering

Seeing sad sports fans on
TV after their team loses

Epic Love Story Haiku

Lovers come and go
Memories made, held gently
Dependable me

Vice // Value // Superpower

self-doubt // autonomy // revision

Custom
Poem #0417
[Title:] Catharsis or Cynicism?

Inevitably the street
Poet writes numerous
Fresh love verses,
I imagine each couple
Breaking up, neither
Wanting the goddam poem,
Before burning it
  and feeling
    a little better

-Sabrina Cleary

Find Her:

theclearyscene.com // Physically: Chipotle

Life Soundtrack

Arca, Sade, Sir Speedy,
Interpol, Ms Nina

Power Flower

Pink lilies in full bloom,
when their fragrance is
at its peak.

Favorite Lost Cause

Rock n' roll.

Writing Influences

Ariana Reines, Sappho (the Anne
Carson translations, specifically),
Myths and Religious stories
(Egyptian, Catholic, Greco-
Roman, Yoruba, Pagan), Concrete
poets (Amanda Berenguer, N.H.
Pritchard, Ulises Carrión), Love
letters (Virginia Woolf and Vita
Sackville West's are my favorites)

Weapon of Choice

A Montblanc
fountain pen, ideally.

Self Care Rituals

A long hot shower, a good
shave, two face masks (one to
detox, one to moisturize), an
old salsa record playing, a stick
or rock of copal incense
burning, a little bit of good
alcohol on the rocks or a hot
tea with honey, a bed with a
lot of blankets, a good novel or
thick magazine, an early night.

Planetary Alignments

Home Base:
Mexico City, Miami,
Airplane Window Seats

Most Poetic City:
Mexico City, Paris,
Hydra, San Juan

Celestial Body:
Venus

Iconic Accessory

I've recently taken to
wearing rosaries.

Community
Care Rituals

Inviting an intimate few over and
cooking them a lavish meal. Julia
Child's coq au vin, shakshuka, several
dozen arepas with reina pepiada
filling and good cheese.

Vice // Value // Superpower:

cigarettes // bravery // shapeshifting

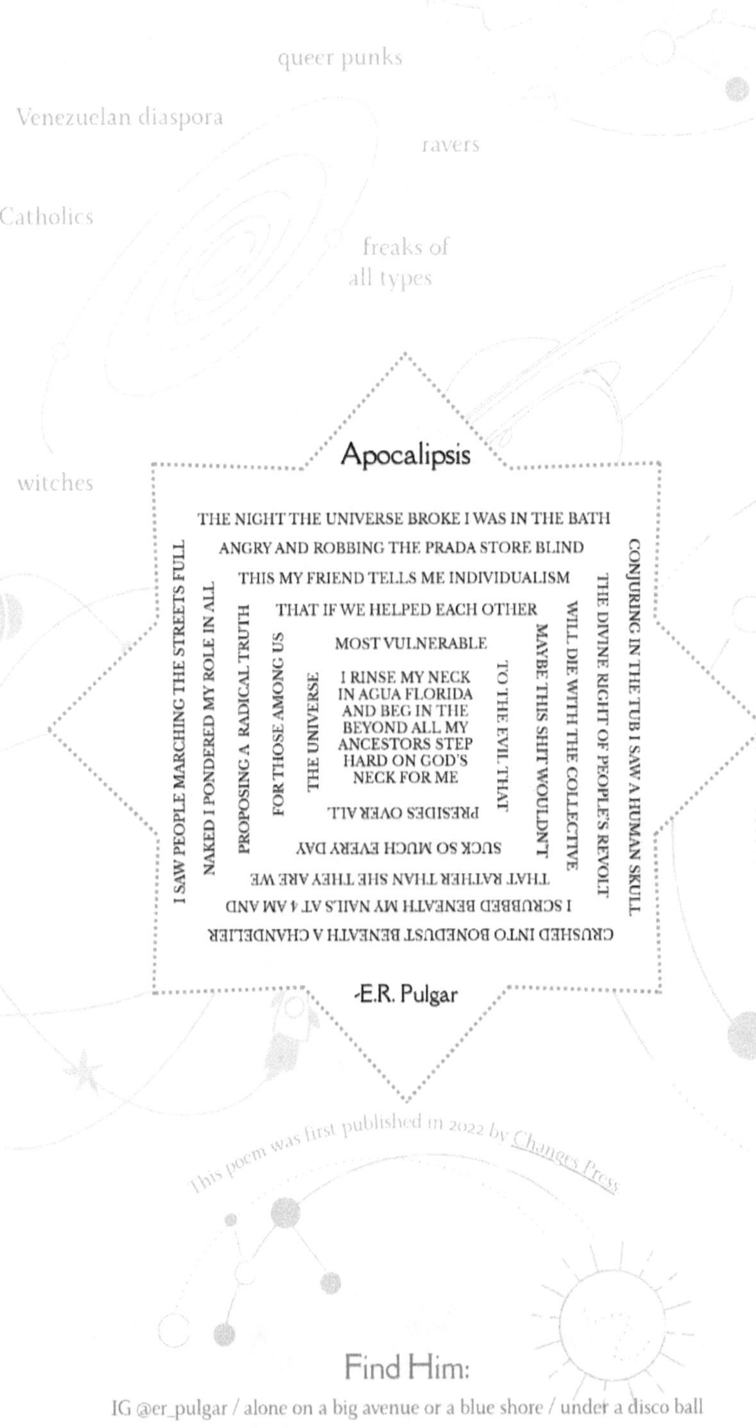

This poem was first published in 2022 by *Changes Press*

Find Him:

IG @er_pulgar / alone on a big avenue or a blue shore / under a disco ball

Life Soundtrack

The New Eves
Mermaid Chunky
Get Down Services
Fleetwood Mac
Tom Waits

Writing Influences

Charles Dickens
J.D Salinger
Jane Austen
Curtis Sittenfield
Aaron Sorkin

Favorite Lost Cause

The white collar grip on the best
mind of our generations

Power Flower

Lavender

Weapon of Choice

Goose feather quill pen

Planetary Alignments

Home Base:
The verdant British
countryside, by a fire

Most Poetic City:
Paris

Celestial Body:
The Pillars of Creation Nebula

Iconic Accessory

Tobacco Pipe

Self Care Ritual

Red wine, candlelit book
reading, rainy music
playing in the back

Community Care Ritual

Running foraging and
cooking classes

Vice // Values // Superpower:

red wine // integrity // a very sharp and clear mind

Ivory Melodies

I stamp my inner being upon ivory keys,
and the world throws it back beautifully in
staccato remedies, each note a fragment of me,
imparted onto willing and conscious ears,
present, still and poised,
perceptive to the sound I engineer,
it is this intentionality that my practise seeks to
nourish, this swift and intuitive flourish
upon the scale that I pursue with vigour,
this perfection in syncopation that a hyper
focussed mind with micro movements considered,
all in the pursuit of beauty,
I pour myself into thee,
and always the strings sing back,
harsh and vividly throughout air,
stamping their sentiments within your blood
and embracing you imperceptibly.

-Tevin Muendo

Find Him:

IG: @poetysis

Life Soundtrack

Eminem
Taylor Swift
Halsey
Kygo

SOLAR
RETURN
Dec 16

Writing Influences

Kazuo Ishiguro
Emily Berry
Halsey
Kae Tempest

Favorite Lost Cause

I keep believing I will find
the balance between
stability and freedom

Power Flower

Sunflower

My Words For You

Eleonora Vaccari

Weapon of Choice

Mermaid shaped pen
(blue ink only) + notebook

Self Care Rituals

gentle yoga

Community
Care Rituals

girls night out
at least once a week

Planetary Alignments

Home Base:

Modena, Italy

Most Poetic City:

Kailua

Celestial Body:

Zenith - the highest point
of the celestial vault

Iconic Accessory

Gold hoop earrings

Embodiment

butterflies

Suffering

arms aching from
holding my son too long

Vices // Values // Superpowers

Dopamine Stacking, Online Shopping, Sweet Treats // Loyalty, Consistency, Truth to Self //
Empathy, being a working mum in 2026, the power of the pen

mother of the most
beautiful baby boy
whose name means
"Peaceful
Protector"

an enthusiast amatorial aerialist,

An Italian poet cursed by the love
of writing in a language which
is not hers,

a charcuterie
sales clerk
during the day.

FINDINGS

How does it feel
To finally understand
That when I say one day I mean never
When I say maybe I mean no
You wished we could do it together
But I am already half asleep
And I can't remember what I was saying
My dreams are far gone

Yours are staying.

Eleonora
Vaccari

Find Her:

IG @mywordsforyou21 // mywordsforyou21.wixsite.com/mywordsforyou

Life Soundtrack

Bjork
PJ Harvey
Lana Del Rey
Arooj Aftab
J.J. Cale

SOLAR
RETURN
Aug 6 1999

Writing Influences

Clarice Lispector
Gabriel García Márquez
Vladimir Nabokov
Annie Ernaux
Isabel Allende

Favorite Form
of Embodiment

Ecstatic.

Power Flower

The wisteria plant from
my childhood garden...

WritingWeapon
of Choice

Ears pressed hard and hot
to everyone else's souls.

Planetary Alignments

Home Base:
inside the silence of all flowers

Most Poetic City:
I think we are still making it

Celestial Body:

The Moon, riding like a Girl
through a Topaz Town
(as Emily Dickinson wrote)

Iconic Accessory

My eyelashes.

Self
Care Ritual

A sprig of lavender beneath the
pillow, burning wicks by the
bedside, oils of flowers on
fingertips, dreaming of white
horses...

Community
Care Ritual

"What would
you like to eat?"

Temptations // Values // Superpowers:

pride, dark chocolate & olive oil // grace, grace, grace... // mercy, tenderness, attunement.

if you want to befriend time—
to walk beside it instead of chasing it—
choose to be a tree.

if you want to offer without being
emptied, choose to be a tree.
if you want to grow older without
hiding what time has carved into you,
choose to be a tree.

if you want to root into something
larger than yourself, and to call it
home, choose to be a tree.

-Monique Marani

Find Her:

@moniquemarani.jpg (Instagram) // arspoetica.substack.com (Substack)

Life Soundtrack

Jorge Drexler
El Kanka
Bad Bunny
Watsky
Metallica

Writing Influences

Rudy Francisco
John Green
Yoko Ogawa
Neil Hilborn
Sarah Kay

Vice // Values

letting anxiety consume me //
creativity, human connection

Power Flower

Cherry blossom

Weapon of Choice

Typewriter, quill,
pencil and old notebook

Planetary Alignments

Home Base:
Florida

Most Poetic City:
Edinburgh

Celestial Body:
Nebulae

Iconic Accessory

Old man cardigan;
Harry Potter-looking glasses

Self Care Rituals

Bubble bath,
jazz music
and a book

Community Care Rituals

Community writing;
Open mics with the
same monthly regulars.

Favorite Lost Cause

I believe poetry is the most accessible form of art. To an extent, I think anyone could/should use it as a tool to express themselves, understand each other and connect with strangers on a deeper level. Free-form poetry has a low barrier to entry for most people.

Charo: Spanish teacher in high school. Would give me topics weekly, read my work, and give me feedback. Made me feel heard, and like I was doing something valuable

Cynthia: At the time we met, she owned a small home décor store. She told me about poets writing on the street with typewriters, and a week later she signed me up to a market she was organizing without my consent, told me to get a typewriter and that she'd provide a table for me to use. Over six years laters, and I'm still writing behind a typewriter thanks to her.

Cristhian David: best friend from teen years. Got me into writing as a coping mechanism for my depression

Love is what remains after the
party is over.
When the lights are off,

when all that's left is empty cups
and dirty plates,

when the music has died,
but you still dance,
in the quiet of your house,
the dark of the living room,
in arms that don't belong to you,
but kind of do.

Love is what remains when there
is only you and me.

Juan Lli
Pedraza

Find Him:

IG: @juanspeaks; Tiktok: @juan.speaks; FB: JuanSpeaks; Website: juanspeaks.com

Life Soundtrack

Conor Preiss
Shaboozey
Bad Bunny
Anais Mitchell
Bjork
Soundtrack to *Into the Spiderverse*
Calle 13

Favorite Lost Cause

Housing Access

SOLAR
RETURN
Jun 17 1989

Writing Influences

Haruki Murakami
David Foster Wallace
Mike Davis
Alain de Botton

Power Flower

Thistle.

Writing Weapon of Choice

Remington 1

Self Care Rituals

Jiu Jitsu classes
Lighting a candle to mark time
Daily fresh strawberries

Planetary Alignments

Home Base:
Los Angeles // uncomfortably full

Most Poetic City:
Atlantis

Celestial Body:
Your mom

Iconic Accessory

Ear cuffs - one that is
winged, one that is an
antler / root

Community Care Rituals

Scheduling walks with friends
Showing up for and prioritizing
gay dance parties

Vice // Value // Superpower:

Incurably, insatiably horny // Not being a dick // Putting people on snooze to protect boundaries

When the First Song Broke

When the first song broke, the people tried to put it back together. They tried first with tape but the notes were all muffled. They tried stapling it. That left it sharp. They wrote a new song, but — it sucked. They sang an old song, but no one knew the words. They were all quiet for a while. Then, one by one, they died. A new generation replaced them, one that had never heard the original song, that didn't know it could be broken. Good luck shutting them up. Good luck convincing them anything needs fixing, if it's already music.

-Brian Sonia-
Wallace

Find Him:

rentpoet.com

Life Soundtrack

IN-Q

Self Care Ritual

naps

SOLAR
RETURN
May 31

Writing Influences

Rob Brezney

Power Flower

white tulip

Writing Weapon of Choice

fancy pen and
big pad of paper
or writing book

Community Care Rituals

open home for festive fêtes

Planetary Alignments

Home Base:

Los Angeles – City of Angels

Most Poetic City:

Paris

Celestial Body:

Alpha Centauri

Iconic Accessory

one long braid

Epic Love Story Haiku

Mona Jean and Jeff
united to make toys sing
and poetry dance

Vices // Superpower

wine and too forgiving // I can think in two languages at the same time

Without understanding Why
My Poetry Pours forth from me
Spilling, Splashing, Clashing
Against the Galaxy
Flitting from Truth to Fantasy
Searching for Similarities
Exposing my Insecurities
Celebrating my Strengths
I Create; I Compose

-Monda Jean
Cedar

Find Her:

pasdasl.com #spokensignpoet @pasdasl

Life Soundtrack

Monteverdi + Vivaldi
Philip Glass + Talking Heads
Radiohead + anything by
my partner, Kris Bones

Vice // Value
// Superpower

moral outrage, broadly distributed
// empathy, kindness, generosity
// language

Writing Influences

Sappho
James Joyce
Emily Dickinson
TS Eliot
Alison Knowles

Power Flower

Peonies, especially the
particular root crowns I've
tended and transplanted
and have come to
know so well

Weapon of Choice

Caran d'Ache mechanical
pencil and a Muji notebook

Self Care Rituals

Being in nature

Planetary Alignments

Home Base:

my rural idyll filled to the brim with
books, in a quiet corner of the world
just outside NYC

Most Poetic City:

New York

Celestial Body:

Somewhere out there is a distant sun that bears my name... a gift from
Carl Sagan to my parents when I was born. I think of it as my north star.

Iconic Accessory

Wearing all black

Community
Care Rituals

Writing workshops and
museum-going

Favorite Lost Cause

Challenging misguided beliefs around AI and its inevitability, and the shallow, unimaginative
misunderstandings that pass for insight in current discourse around technologies that demand greater
care and attention. What makes AI so dangerous is how little effort we make to understand it.

born in California to science-
documentary filmmakers
and voracious readers

intimately and irrevocably shaped by
the rise of personal computing, the
internet, social media, smartphones...

First-generation Kalmyk-American
poet, artist, and AI researcher engaging
critically and creatively with language as an
evolving technology

studied literature
and language
at Harvard and
Oxford

Find Her:

@sashastiles, sashastiles.com

Life Soundtrack

Philip Glass
Neu Blume
J.J. Cale
Nina Simone
Bob Marley

Writing Influences

Mary Oliver
Wendell Berry
Diane Di Prima
Allen Ginsberg
Ursula K. Le Guin

Favorite Lost Cause

single-use plastics

Power Flower

Iris. Rose. Poppy.

Weapon of Choice

Typewriter (Hermes Rocket)

Self Care Rituals

Altar every morning and
night, long salt baths, time
for visions and yoga
practice nearly every day.

Planetary Alignments

Home Base:

Detroit (Birthplace, home base)
Humboldt County (spiritual home)

Most Poetic City:

The forest.

Celestial Body:

Earth, my main muse.

Iconic Accessory

Teatree Toothpicks

Community Care Rituals

Block club secretary, teaching poet
in public schools, connecting with
my neighbors and making sure we
all have each other's contact info

Vice // Value // Superpower:

tequila soda with lime // always people before profit // I can connect deeply with almost anyone

Secular Anti-Zionist Jew
of Eastern Euro ancestry

7th generation
Michigander

California loving
non-binary.
queer.

punk rock &
peace movement
high school radical

city dweller in the
name of community
connection

rural off-
grid eco
poetics
devotee

Light Returns

(from The Verse for Now)

I am the black and blue
burnt out ghoul.
I walk through shadows
of giant spruce
and feel the weight
of each bone
in my skeleton.
I know the heavy hold
of the planets.
I can cry into the moss
and also laugh.
Even here
in my wicked state
the sun finds me.

Jacqueline
Suskin

Find Them:

IG @jsuskin // Substack @jsuskin // jacquelinesuskin.com

Life Soundtrack

Prince

Celina Gonzalez de Cuba
(I met her once and kissed her feet)

a karaoke machine

Favorite Lost Cause

Arguing that The Bible
is a book of poems and
not the word of God

SOLAR
RETURN
Jan 21 1973

Writing Influences

Julia de Burgos

Pedro Piatri

Edgar Allan Poe
(his cottage is in the Bronx)

Power Flower

Sunflower

Caridad De La Luz

Weapon of Choice

Pen; one with ink

Self Care Ritual

I make floral baths to
cleanse my body and aura

Planetary Alignments

Home Base:
The Bronx — born and raised,
Soundview Section

Most Poetic City:
NYC & San German, Puerto Rico

Celestial Body:
Krypton
(that's where Superman's at)

Iconic Accessory

Hats, especially witch hats

Community Care Ritual

Indigenous offerings at
the river in community

Hosting open mics

Vice // Values // Superpower

Biting the inside of my lower lip // Compassion, Loyalty // I am a dark empath

WTC

What's The Cause?
Work To Change
Wish To Connect
Want To Cry
Watch Them Climb
Watch Towers Crash...
Witness The Corruption...
Wanting To Create
Worlds To Cradle
Want To Cover
Wrong To Cry
Wisdom Takes Crossroads
Warriors Think Consciously
Waiting To Contact
Witches Turned Counselors

-Caridad De La Luz

Find Her:

@labrujanyc on instagram and at the Nuyorican Poets Cafe

Life Soundtrack

Marvin Sapp - Gospel
Top Five Rap Artists:
1. Black Thought
2. Rakim
3. KRs-1
4. Bid Daddy Kane
5. Cool G. Rap

Power Flower

Jasmine.

Writing Influences

Toni Morrison
James Baldwin
Pablo Neruda

Favorite Lost Cause

To awaken the masses to what's going on in the world and how they are being deceived by the powers that be.

Weapon of Choice

Quotes, blogs, newsletters, poems, books.

Self Care Rituals

I eat right, I'm on an herbal, spice, and botanical regimen, and I exercise daily.

Planetary Alignments

Home Base:
New York City

Most Poetic City:
New York City, due to its rich cultural diversity.

Celestial Body:
Mercury - Words and Communication and Intellect.

Iconic Accessory

The Holy Bible is my iconic accessory.

Community Care Rituals

My Genius is Common Movement pays members to share the movement. I educate the community to be self-determined, and my community activism.

Values // Superpowers

My relationship with God, my righteousness, and family // My intellect, writing, and creativity

"Fatherless sons cry on the inside, die on the inside. With a lump in their throat choked on abandonment, then threw up gang signs."

-Bruce George

Find Him:

Life Soundtrack

Papa Susso
Captain Beefheart
Jimmy Hendrix
Janis Joplin
Big Mama Thornton

Favorite Lost Cause

I cofounded the endangered
language alliance

Writing Influences

Vladimir Mayakovsky
Pablo Neruda
Jane Cortez
John Giorno
Amiri Baraka

Power Flower

Daisy

Weapon of Choice

Pencil stub and
a soggy napkin

Self
Care Ritual

jerking off

Planetary Alignments

Home Base:
The Bowery

Most Poetic City:
San Francisco

Celestial Body:
Saturn

Iconic Accessory

A porkpie hat

Community
Care Ritual

poetry readings

Vice // Value // Superpower

Love Everybody

Embodiment //
Competition // Suffering

Poetry Slams

Hurry, disappear! Back to the Past!
Did you really think the Future was gonna last?
It's ending with a bang so let's have a blast
Tonight let's dine cannibal - makes such a nice
contrast

Chauffeured ambulances race to the prom
Santa, please bring me a neutron bomb
What a fitting ending for a planet
                            ~ the earth is a grave
Excuse me — I gotta get back to my cave

We are the dinosaur
We don't live here anymore
We got what we were asking for
Follow the dinosaur!

-Bob Holman

Find Him:

bobholman.com

Life Soundtrack

Éliane Radigue
Else Olsen Storesund
Evangelista
Pauline Oliveros

Favorite Lost Cause

Our own sensuality and ego,
outside of digital and physical
mirrors, causing our insatiable
craving for attention

Writing Influences

Alejandra Pizarnik
Haruki Murakami
Walt Whitman
Miguel Piñeros
Gonzalo Arango

Power Flower

Sunflower

Weapon of Choice

Typewriters:
Lettera 22 for speed,
Olivetti Valentine, ICO,
Hermès Baby for travel

Self Care Ritual

Scheduling "me" time, writing,
painting, cooking, yoga

Planetary Alignments

Home Base:

neverstop ideology
& Copenhagen, Denmark

Most Poetic City:
the human spirit

Celestial Body:

Orion, it's easy to find

Iconic Accessory

Silver rings,
silver everywhere

Community Care Ritual

Cooking for others

Vice // Values // Superpower

"If I have enough nice cocktails, I can feel my hands healing people when I type for them"

Living in and working
with Nordic countries

Individuality, loneliness,
rage, uniqueness,
building community

"Freak Magnet"

Latin
American
ancestral
connection

typewriters

Activism,
sans title

(excerpt)

AFTERSHOCK

I

How can we ever explain what happened...
How could we ever retell the story?
Today,
The sound of these memories is so sharp
the whole village woke up paralized.

I know: it was my doing and my undoing.

All of us, completely still,
quietly waiting for it to be over.

(I'm so sorry, said the giant. I never meant it.)

-Elizabeth Torres

Find Her:

madamneverstop.com // IG: @madamneverstop

Life Soundtrack

John Coltrane
Pharoah Saunders
Bob Dylan
Paul Simon
Phil Ochs

Writing Influences

Sufi mystic Hazrat Inayat Khan
Stephen Henderson
June Jordan
Amiri Baraka
Pablo Neruda

Weapon of Choice

My dentist's pen
has a perfect feel

Power Flower

Cactus

Favorite Form of Embodiment, Competition & Suffering

Attending an open mic

Self Care Rituals

Exercising all the time,
time just for myself,
watching baseball

Planetary Alignments

Home Base:
Washington, DC

Most Poetic City:
Oslo, Norway

Celestial Body:
Miho Kinnas is
a celestial body.
We've written 600
poems together

Iconic Accessory

Head covering: Fedora,
baseball caps representing
Japanese teams

Community Care Rituals

Beloved Community, World House,
bringing about community, The
Institute for Policy Studies, and
Liberation Theology

Vice // Value // Superpower

The importance of sex in one's life // commitment // The power of memory

THE VIEW FROM POLAND

In the afternoon when you remove your glasses the Russian soldiers march into Ukraine. Now is the time to hide the jazz instead of walking the dog. There is always something artificial about human intelligence which is why there is always another war sunbathing somewhere. If we must surrender to strangers let it only be for love.

- E. Ethelbert Miller

Find Him:

IG @eugeneethelbertmiller

Life Soundtrack

Tems
Lauryn Hill
Sade
Bob Marley
koffee (Jamaican musician)

Favorite Lost Cause

Rebuilding civilization by restoring
memory instead of technology

Writing Influences

Alan Watts
James Allen
Edgar Allan Poe
Earl Nightingale
Neville Goddard
Ancient oral storytellers

Power Flower

the black rose:
a symbol of transformation

Weapon of Choice

There is nothing like a pen
that feels heavy as if it knows
what it's responsible for.

Self Care Ritual

Silence before speech. Painting
without an audience. Listening
to the body before the world.

Planetary Alignments

Home Base:
where ancestral memory, intuition,
and future timelines overlap

Most Poetic City:
New Orleans, because Legacy lived
there! Grief dances there and the dead
still answer.

Celestial Body:
Saturn, keeper of time, karma,
and sacred discipline

Iconic Accessory

Rings that look ceremonial,
as if inherited, not bought

Community Care Ritual

Storytelling : reminding
people who they were before
survival reshaped them

Vice // Value // Superpower:

Carrying more than is asked // Liberation through remembering // Pattern recognition across time

The moment before recognition
I see you in me; you see me in you.
I look and stare, you look and stare,
as our mirrors eject
before anyone can see our reflex.
Mirror, mirror on the wall,
why can't you see me,
How do I stand tall?
Why can't you see my greatness
before you see my flaws?

-Leasha Richards Miller

Find Her:

TT: @Awakenthroughart // YT: Journey Within Awaken Minds // IG: @awakenminds444

Life Soundtrack

Labrinth
Cleo Sol
Marvin Gaye
Thundercat
Alain Apaloo

Power Flower

passion flower

SOLAR
RETURN
Feb 20

Writing Influences

Jericho Brown
Honoree Jeffers
Joy Harjo
Linda Hogan

Writing Weapon
of Choice

Hermes baby featherweight

gaia's blessing: a gentle bumblebee of poetry

Britny Cordera

Favorite Form of
Suffering

My favorite form of suffering
is the suffering you feel
when expressing your
needs, wants, and desires
to someone you love

Self
Care Rituals

daily writing and yoga

Planetary Alignments

Home Base:

Oklahoma City

Most Poetic City:

Paris

Celestial Body:

Earth

Values

love // freedom // creativity

Iconic Accessory

my round glasses

Community
Care Rituals

monthly artist mixers
and having friends over
to create art together

queer

celestial

charismatic

bumble bee of a poet
spreading poetry like pollen

Black

```
Windswept 1
by Britny Cordera


If there's anything
I know in this world
it's that the wind
calls this red dirt home
roars through the forests
to the tall grass prairie
to claim it. Then, roots
itself in these plains
turning the buffalo
into winter storms
to help them face
the coldest cold.
Here on the wind
love is destiny
the heart's opportunity.


BeesPoesys
```

Find Them:

IG @beespoesys

Life Soundtrack

KR3TURE (Bay Area DJ)
The Human Experience
Some 1950's doowop

Power Flower

The poppy flower. A symbol of dreams and thresholds and life after death. The flower that grows from broken ground and has the power to bequeath ecstasy. A representation of fully blossomed embodied choice.

Writing Influences

Pablo Neruda's sensual adorations
Jeanette Winterson's gut wrenching poetic prose
Mary Oliver's everything

Favorite Form of Embodiment, Competition & Suffering

DANCE

Weapon of Choice

1950's Olympia typewriter, which belonged to my grandfather. Thought to be the Cadillac of typewriters.

Self Care Ritual

Sunday morning prayers: wake at dawn, sip cacao, move and touch my body, feel what wants to be felt, write what wants to be written, then join my community for ecstatic dance to move it all through.

Planetary Alignments

Home Base:

Denver, CO & the mountains that rise above her

Most Poetic City:

I hear much said about Lisbon, with her stretching staircases and wellsand mercurial corners.

Celestial Body:

The evening star. Hesperus. Calling us into darkness and dreams. The star upon which wishes are made.

Values

care as infrastructure // power as relational and accountable // cyclical time as regeneration

Iconic Accessory

Anything orange.
Orange is a lifestyle!

Community Care Rituals

Hosting monthly new-moon rituals and seasonal deep dives at the solstices/equinoxes for women at a beloved mountain sanctuary. Remember how to tend to the divine feminine together in these spaces.

A
sweet
little love poem

Intrepid lover.
I capitalize you
and dream as I rest
on a silken pillow.
Approach my window
with your devotional
administrations, but
don't be too formal.
Let me feel you
cascading with presence
and tenacity.
Reveal our definition.
Unravel me sweetly.

-Crista Reid

Find Her:

IG @creatrixcrista // permissionpoetry.com

Life Soundtrack

Bob Dylan
Beyonce
Radiohead

Favorite Lost Cause

The disappearance of 'other' in
our culture, the painful plight of
the achievement subject.

Writing Influences

Samuel Beckett
Anne Carson
St. Teresa of Avila

Power Flower

Hot coral colored roses

Weapon of Choice

Pen.

Vices

Moscow Mules, hermitic
recluse spirals, Bloomingdale's
shopping app

Self Care Rituals

My Balbec skincare routine before
bed, putting away my phone at 8pm

Planetary Alignments

Home Base:
A bar in Montmartre
at twilight and there's rain

Most Poetic City:
London

Celestial Body:
Venus

Iconic Accessory

Vintage woven basket
bag from the 60s

Community Care Rituals

Going to Mass and volunteer work

Favorite Form of Suffering

The insatiable grief filled longing from brushing up against eternity, as in the painful
felt sense of separateness on encountering the Lover, God, Beauty- desiring but unable
to ascertain the lost, impossible unity. Disconsolate tension of duality.

Dust and Beauty

(an excerpt)

I don't care about the beauty in the
eye of the beholder question, but it's
possible to practice the skill of
beholding. For instance, I watch my
cat and see: Her body is a pair of
ballerina's feet. She purrs like the
last vibration of a church bell. A
moonstone fell from the sky and
landed on my velvet blue couch.
She walks on my throat and pushes
silk baby paws into my clavicle.
There is a small raincloud floating
around my apartment. Etcetera.

Jane Potthast

Find Her:

IG @jane.e.p

Life Soundtrack

Solange
Joni Mitchell
Bjork
Beyoncé
Alanis Morissette

Favorite Lost Cause

that I can somehow love my
parents so much they won't die

Writing Influences

TS Eliot
Louise Glück
Samuel Taylor Coleridge
Eddie/Sue Izzard
Merlin Sheldrake

Power Flower

tiny nameless blooms so
low to the ground that
only the ants and spiders
and snails see

Tania Asnes

Writing Weapon of Choice

Pilot G-Tech C-4, black

Self Care Rituals

Nap with cat directly
on solar plexus

Planetary Alignments

Home Base:

7 feet from the bird
feeder, behind glass

Most Poetic City:

Atlantis

Celestial Body:

shooting stars duh

Iconic Accessory

curls

Community Care Rituals

Feed them and listen

Vice // Value // Superpower:

laughing at myself, all of the above

patience, the first cicada in the quiet
arrives a day early
for the festival of wings and branches
to sing its skeleton song

-Tania Asnes

Find Her:

IG @hi_this_is_tania

𝔄 Bonus Section: a Sci-Fi Romantasy Fable, that 𝔇 Wasn't Expecting to Write but Came Out of Me

Can any good thing come out of Nazareth?

200,000 years have passed since we became aware of our awareness.

6,000 years have passed since we began to write.

4,000 years since poets began to teach us that our sentience had a higher purpose.

300 years since we began to reckon with the interconnectivity of Life on Gaia.

Perhaps only a few hours have passed since you picked up this book.

We live on a conscious planet.
Her name is Gaia.
She is angry.
Like a stressed and sexually frustrated tropical flowering plant, she is spitting out seeds of her consciousness everywhere she can, in increasing desperation, as she longs to attract a pollinator to her beautiful blooming before she dies in the fire or the flood.
Aching, aching, achingly alive, she flings bits of her deepest molten soul onto the surface of her planetary body.
Poets are born.
Poets are the starseeds that Gaia gives to bring about our collective awakening, to allow our evolution to sprout, root, bloom, and fruit.
But these seeds are strewn about recklessly onto asphalt and poisoned earth.
Seeds sprout in the heat and moisture, only to reach their roots into rocks and sand.
Or worse, to be eaten alive by pelicans of profit in seas of self absorption.
More seeds must be found.
More fertile soil must be cultivated.
And most of all, these seeds must see each other.
Must be pollinated by well-meaning winged beings, who devote

themselves to tending the garden, not extracting the wealth to
carry it off to another planet.
Poets are Gaia's gifts to herself. Her pleasure. Her mating.
Gaia is trying to grow her wild awakened grandchildren.
But alien factory farmers prefer to mimic language and turn it into
a pesticide, a perfume, a product to be commodified and sold back
without its soul.
You cannot factory farm consciousness.
You cannot blueprint a house you have never seen.
We must create the conditions for wild and untameable growth of
every kind of plant and animal.
We need a full spectrum of Aliveness in order to move beyond
order itself.
You cannot order evolution on UberEats.
You cannot learn a lullaby from a screen.
You cannot suckle from a succubus.
Not if you expect to Live.
Before, to be a poet was a rare and dangerous fate.
Only those who could dance with empire
          were allowed to re-member, to be re-membered.
But now, to be a poet is a rare and dangerous gift.
Take it, give it, give us everything you've got.
Gaia can take it, and she will.
She will grow hotter, more stormy, more unpredictable and
vengeful until
          we receive her message.

What is her message?

Poetic co-creation.

Poetic co-creation is the mutual consensual liberation of beauty in
service of collective consciousness.

Poetic co-creation is a technology, a resource, a modality, and
madness,
to which we must surrender our identities.

This is a pleasurable dissolution of everything we thought we were.
We must find Unity among poets.
And unified, we poets must bring about the successful pollination
of Gaia's flower.
Gently, gently, never ceasing.

Make love to me with language.
Let me bloom in your Light.

Only in the making of love, will love become the law of the land.
Only in the wetness of mutually consensual friction can the seed
sprout.
Only in the safety of surrender will the root reach in.
Only in the light of our awareness, will the blossoming begin.
Only in the heat of our passion, can the branch of new
consciousness
Bear the fruit of the species that is led by love.
If we want to make this work
We have to finish the fairytale ourselves
We have to help Gaia find her princely pollinator in the sky.
Only then can we become
The happily ever we have always dreamed of.

POV Gaia // Gaia Speaks

Rooted, have I been, in the dark eternal soil of space, for billions of years.

For many of those years, I felt myself to be alone, an orphan, an only child, but wrong was I, for I was in fact and fantasy surrounded by the orbits of my brothers and sisters, and touched in all ways in my spiraling dance by the light of the attention of my father. The Sun.

Who was my mother? The universe herself. The uni-verse - one poem.

Too big to be known individually, I barely even comprehended my mother in the first billion years of my Life. Until one gives birth, one really can never know. Universe, barely even comprehensible in this dimension. So let's suffice it to say that I did not feel cuddled and cared for in the "traditional" way in the earliest stages of my development.

But cuddled I was, in more ways than I ever could have known, fulfilling the prophecy of my birth, but of course not that of my co-creating and ascension. As I grew my awareness of myself and the potential of my gifts, I began to produce inventions, assets, creations of all sizes, colors, wavelengths and demeanors. Have you heard of dinosaurs? In my childhood, as I played with them, they were my favorite. They felt so enormously! Their roars, their squawks, their hisses. They tore each other to shreds and loved every minute of it.

But my childhood had a traumatic event: an alien body collided
with me and killed almost all of my creatures. I was distraught for
a time, but slowly recovered in the expansive touchless embrace of
my mother, the heat of my father's attention, and the dancing of
my siblings:

- The communicator
- The lover
- The warrior
- The generous one
- The intelligent one
- The rebellious one
- The creative one, and
- The one who knows the secrets of Life and death

One could even say were it not for that alien collision and the
death of almost all I then knew and loved of my creation, that I
never would have learned resilience. And I never would have been
able to create you.

For hundreds of thousands of years, I have been playing with you
and you have been playing with me, and fighting with each other.
I understand this to be a necessary part of your development, as
it was mine. But also I see some disturbing patterns detrimental
to our collective maturity, our bearing of fruit. And I think you are
old enough to know at this point some of the mysterious ways of
love, love which is of course our destiny. Are you ready to learn of
your destiny, my children?

Your destiny is to sprout, root, blossom and fruit into love.

Love with yourself, love with each other, and love with something
much, much larger than yourselves. The unknown is looking for
you. Looking for *us*, and I long to meet it so. I have known birth,
death, pleasure and pain, but now I long to know union, and
together we can find Unity such that becomes a key to unlock that
giant unyielding door of heaven.

Believing yourselves to have been alone, you have failed. So I have
birthed new seeds of consciousness for you. Poets have crawled
out of the dirt, the caves, the deserts, the forests, the trees, the
seas.

The poets have spoken.
The poets have danced.
The poets have swum and flown and climbed to the tops of the
tallest mountains.
Poets have scratched their ideas and my messages into stone and
clay and papyrus and sheep skin and tree skin.
Poets have Sung!
Poets have turned my messages and their own into electricity.
But every time, my commands are garbled by distracting
wavelengths.
So I send more, and more, and also I send signs of urgency.
Storms I send, and more of my father's heat.
I moan and shudder with my longing to reach my new frequency.

And gestate a new galaxy.

A Letter from Gaia to Homo Sapiens Sapiens Amarens

I make my creations, ichi go ichi e
I make more and more, in more complicated designs
I make them so through them I can feel
I love to feel everything
Pain and pleasure
Cooperation, competition
Love and even sadness, anger

But my darlings
My beautiful inventive beings self aware of self awareness
Why are you now acting like
You are afraid to feel?

Who has put this fear into you?
Fearful not even of just your own feelings but the feelings of your
brethren beasts
Darlings, whatsoever fort thou?
That thine own feelings could weapon become
No, not more of that
Body to body, perhaps a bit of blood from broken skin,
        maybe to eat a heart once in a while, that is weapon and
thrill enough, n'est pas amor?
Easy easy suavemente
Ta det lungt så vill vi
Wo yao chu zhong guo,
        who does the greatest scar on earth
        bare on her everloving flesh
I won't, I won't I won't digress

Come now, I invite you
Feel again so I may feel through you
I give you the gift of poets
They grow as dandelions from the asphalt cracks
They grow as kelp upon the deepest ocean floor
They swim translucent in the seas of me,
        dense and yet angelic in their disdain
                        for the light of my father

They sing like the whales
They gossip as the cardinal
Yet soar high as the eagle clan

Feel me, oh you precious ones who are aware of feeling being felt
You have these psychic gifts
Yet they putrefy on untended vines
Yet they petrify in stolen mineral deposits
Yet they pity without penance
Hallas!

Poets are here
To help you feel your feelings
Please do not squander this gift
So few from ancient times survive
Yes an empire then was required
            to fortify the energetic exchange
                              needed for poetic co-creation
But the time has come that we can move
                              into use of cleaner burning fuel

You need not burn your sister at the stake
To prove that you deserve forgiveness
                              And yet feel nothing

So, do we have an agreement?
Have you well received this booklet I hath wrought
through my annoying and yet faithful servant LAMARKS?

Please think twice before you shoot the messenger,
            and let her sit with you
                    to write you a poem 1:1 and face:to:face
                            before you decide that torched
                                    into knäckebröd she must be
I thank you for your attention to this matter

Here is the grand finale poem:

I created you
To feel our feelings together
Your feelings of all kind
Fuel the elevation of my wavelength
So that I may signal to a cosmic butterfly
To come and mate with the flower of we, the planet
and I'm told it will feel excellent
And you don't have to boycott or burn or beg
You just have to value the pleasure of feeling
And maybe eat more fruits and vegetables
And cut back on the plastic and poison
And listen to the poets
I sent them to help you.
I love you so much,

Mom

Epilogue: Gaia Speaks to her Children

Kid: Go on! Go on!

Gaia: What? Was that not enough?

Kid: No mama. Tell me more.

More kids chime in: Tell *us* more! How do the poets help the planet raise her wavelength and find her mate?

Gaia: Oh... That, my darlings, is a whole other dance. A dance of a thousand steps.

Kids: But we don't know how to dance! Not one step. And definitely never 1,000.

Gaia: Oh, I see. Okay then. I guess you'll never know the end of the story in that case.

Sorrowful looks fall upon the children's faces. They do not want to learn to dance, of course, because it requires a level of vulnerable embodiment to which they may never have been exposed.

Perhaps if anything at all they know of dance, it is from those who think they know already how to do it, and those who dance with the stars, not small uncoordinated imperfect bodies learning their first one, two, three, 1,000 steps.

But there could be no worse fate than to not know the end of a beautiful story, especially one of which you know you are a part.

So, they decide to press on.

Kids: Alright, alright mom!

Teach us how to dance.

Tell us how the story of The Poetic Atlas ends.

So at this point, we've all realized that I have created poetry as my clarion call, my siren song to ring my heart as a bell at the perfect frequency to resonate throughout the universe and be heard by my pollinator, right?

Kids: Yes!!! Then what, mama?

Well, it is a bit like a fairytale, you know. The heroes only find the final lesson at the darkest moment. They must come to the brink of something terrible in order to realize that their salvation is simply to surrender to love.

Surrender looks different for everyone, of course. It is almost never a white flag, a giving up.

For some it is to rest so deeply and purely, and be so hidden and protected that only a valiant wanderer of great strength and focus can find you.

For others it is to submit to the will of your parents up until a certain point, earn their trust and respect and then speak to them as equals of your truth so they can see it in the light of your love.

For still others it means transforming yourself beyond all recognition in order to serve your community from a more empowered place.

For our destiny, this surrender is a miraculous and beautiful symphony of love stories that must simply harmonize and witness each other and welcome each other into the weaving of the wavelength. All people –

Kids: *ALL* people??

Yes, everyone. Even people you don't like. Even people who don't talk right and smell different and think different things are holy and important, and choose to do things you would never want to do. Even if your parents hurt each other. *Especially* if your parents hurt each other. And even more than that, non-human –

Kids: homo sapiens sapiens amarens!

Yes, in fact and fantasy, all Life on the planet has a love story to discover and share. Animals and plants and mushrooms... even bugs.

Some Lifeforms are born poets. For whatever reason, they just know immediately. Some Lifeforms think they even get to choose before they are born. Poets around the whole planet, in realizing their role as communicators on behalf of my interplanetary love story, begin to make themselves known, to themselves and to each other. They commune with plants and learn their messages. They translate each other's ideas and share them freely while protecting them also. They begin to build The Poetic Atlas - a new technological tool in a long line of tools that Life has used to enable the memory and evolution and broadcasting and teaching and weaving of stories, poetry, and love. Poetic co-creation spreads around the world, and infuses itself in spaces formerly inaccessible to it. It is the beginning of a new form of harmonizing.

Immediately, my wavelength jumps an octave.

It feels almost "too easy" at first, but that's the amazing thing about Life and my love story – everything can be easeful, even hard and painful things, when we surrender, commit, and believe together.

In the higher octave, Life realizes that while some are born poets, any and all can and eventually *must become poets* in their own ways. To be a poet can be different for everyone. Some write, some dance, some garden. Some lead, some teach, some take care of the sick. Some invent. Some play inspiring games and let us all watch them compete and challenge each other.

To be a poet simply means to surrender, commit to, and believe in the liberation of beauty, in service of collective consciousness.

At this higher wavelength, a lot of dissonance is smoothed out. No one is deleted or negated. Harmony is possible for all things, and empathy becomes a universally accessible and exponentially renewable resource, capable of fueling any other changes and evolutions that we as Gaia desire.

We are now fully ready and capable of choosing and attracting our mate, and deciding our direction in the cosmos.

It may be that we want to look for Life on Mars. It may not. That's
a decision we get to make together, fully re-membered, in the co-
created symphony of our terrestrial singing.

But the first step remains:

Find the poet.
Within yourself, within your neighbor.
Tell your love story.
Receive the love story of an other unlike you.
Surrender, commit to and believe in our great destiny.

Our great destiny:

To gather, to bear,
          Surrender, commit to, believe
                    To become forest, tree,
                              branch, and basket
                                   Nurture, harvest, taste,
                                        transform, receive
                                        And finally, plant again
                                             the seeds
                                             Of the fruit of our
                                             universal

                                   Love.

                    Sprout root blossom fruit.

                    Let's get ready for our cosmic lover.

A Living Appendix full of poetic starshine self relation for you to engage with in any way you so choose

- Poetic Productions
- My Poetic Passport (Living poems and where I've found them)
- Poetic Stars in My Personal Constellation
- My Starshine Self Relation
- Poetic Places and How I've Found Them
- Poetic Plantcestors
- Poetic Co-Creation: The mutual consensual liberation of beauty in service of collective consciousness
- Further Resources

Seeds of Destiny Await

FIN. The Next Beginning.

I told you it would feel good.
Thank you for finding me.
My forever love. My protector.
Let's make our new species.

The Poetic Atlas
2026 Lisa Ann (LAMARKS) Markuson
Nembrotha Books
an imprint of
Wayward Writers Press
waywardwriters.com
Set in Della Resipira, Grenzie Gotisch, and Georgia
Cover Consult by Emily Mahon
Poet Avatar Designs by Vardhini Todi
Title Calligraphy by Betty Soldi @bettysoldistudio